TEN WAYS TO HEAR SNOW

Written by CATHY CAMPER   Illustrated by KENARD PAK

Kokila

To all my Lebanese family, especially my Lebanese aunties, who
encouraged my love of books.
–C. C.

To my dear aunt, Joung Ok Song.
–K. P.

KOKILA
An imprint of Penguin Random House LLC, New York

Text copyright © 2020 by Cathy Camper
Illustrations copyright © 2020 by Kenard Pak

Visit us online at penguinrandomhouse.com

Library of Congress Cataloging-in-Publication Data is available.

Printed in China
ISBN 9780399186332

7 9 10 8

Design by Jasmin Rubero
Text set in Aleo

The art for this book was created digitally.

When Lina woke up, everything was quiet.

No cars honked.

No buses chugged.

No garbage trucks gulped trash across the street.

SNOW!

Last night's blizzard was gone, leaving the city muffled and white.

But today was grape leaf day, when Lina would help her grandma make warak enab. Sitti was losing her eyesight, and Lina loved helping her cook.

"I want to tell Sitti about the snowstorm and make sure she's OK."

"The snow's so deep!" Lina's mom said.
"We could go with you," Lina's dad offered.
But Lina wanted to go to Sitti's by herself.
"Stay warm, habibti," her dad told her.

Lina bundled up.

Outside, the sun on the snow was as bright white as a light bulb. Lina squinched her eyes and pulled her scarf over her nose. She could barely see.

I wonder if this is how Sitti feels, Lina thought. The world sounded softer, but the noises she heard were clearer.

Scraaape, scrip, scraaape, scrip.

What was that?

It was Mrs. Watson's shovel digging out the sidewalk.

That's one way to hear snow, Lina thought.

Lina walked down the street.

Snyak, snyek, snyuk.

The noise was low to the ground. What was that?
It was the treads of Lina's boots crunching snow into tiny
waffles. Two ways to hear snow.

Lina ducked under a pine tree.

Ploompf!

A powdery sound!
A blue jay on a branch had knocked down snow.
Three ways to hear snow, Lina counted. She listened
for more.

Swish-wish, swish-wish.

What was that soft, whiskery noise?
People were sweeping snow off their cars. Their brushes
made the fourth way to hear snow.

Lina cut across the park.

Scritch, scratch, scritch, scratch.

Another snow noise?
Lina saw long, skinny tracks by her boots. Ahead of her,
people were skiing. Their skis made the fifth way to hear snow.

Rachid and Mariam were building a snowman.

Pat, pat, pat.

What was that?
It was mittens smoothing the snowman's head.
The gentle sound made the sixth way to hear snow.

As Lina walked away, her friends whispered and laughed.

Thwomp!

Oh no!
Lina ran away fast from the seventh way to hear snow.

Lina reached Sitti's building
all out of breath, her boots covered
with white powder.

Stomp, stomp, stomp.
Lina giggled. *She* was making the
eighth way to hear snow.

"Hello, Lina," the lady in the lobby said. "Go on in." She pointed toward Lina's grandma's room.

Lina tapped on the door.

"Surprise, Sitti! It's me! I came to make grape leaves with you!"

Lina threw her coat and mittens on the radiator to dry.
"Wonderful! The lamb and rice are ready," Sitti said.

"Yalla, I can't wait!" Lina shouted. "Let's get started."

Lina rinsed the grape leaves and placed them on towels.

"Put some filling in the center, roll them up, and put them in the pot," Sitti instructed.

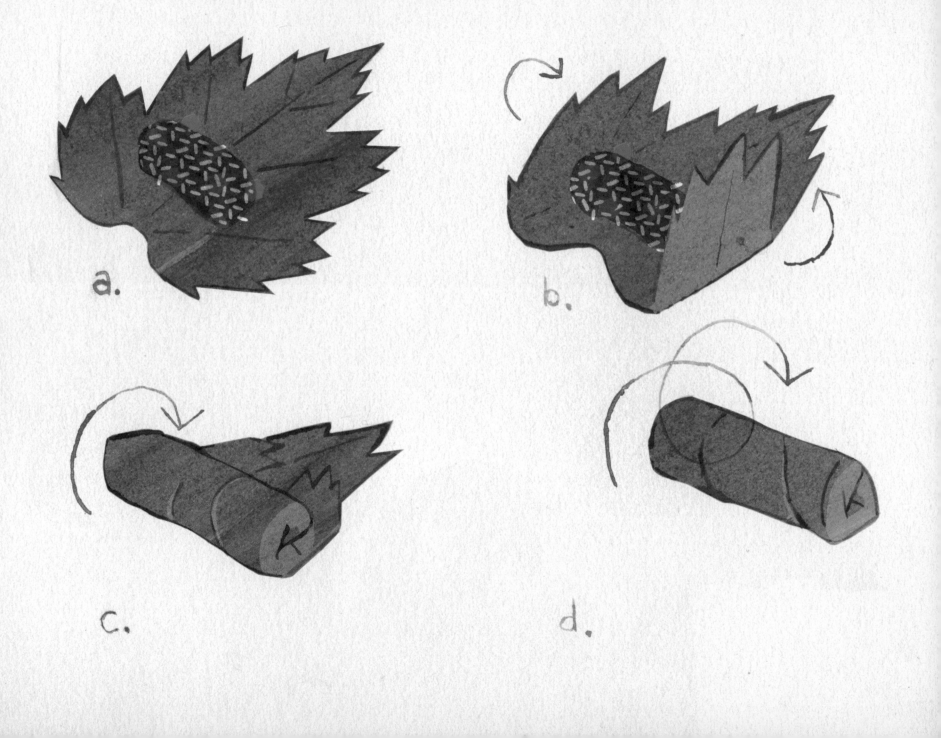

a.

b.

c.

d.

"They're like little grape leaf cocoons,"
Lina said, looking at them piled on the plate.
"Or lots of little sleeping bags,"
Sitti replied.

"Ha! Mine looks like a mustache!" Lina held her stuffed grape leaf under her nose.

Sitti held hers under her nose too. "That's good!" She wrinkled up her face and said, "We look like a coupla real tough guys," in a tough-guy voice.

"Sitti, did you know we had a blizzard last night?"

"Of course."

Lina was surprised. How could her grandma know, when she couldn't see very well?

Then she heard a noise.

Drip, drip went the mittens. It was the sound of snow melting. Nine ways to hear snow!

Suddenly, Lina understood how Sitti knew.

"Sitti, did you *hear* the snow?"

Sitti smiled. "Each morning I open the window and listen. Today everything sounded hushed and soft. No noise is the sound that means it's snowing."

"Sitti, I listened too. I heard snow nine different ways. Shovels were one, boots were two, the blue jay was three . . . "

"Slow down, habibti. I want to hear them all. But right now, shhh . . . "
Sitti went to the window and opened it again.

"Listen," she said.

Outside, the late blue afternoon was completely still.

"Quiet is the tenth way to hear snow."